Chrysanthemum

by Kevin Henkes

VIKING

For Ava

Watercolour paints and a black pen
were used for the full-colour art.

VIKING

Published by the Penguin Group
Penguin Books Ltd, 27 Wrights Lane, London W8 5TZ, England
Penguin Books USA Inc., 375 Hudson Street, New York, New York 10014, USA
Penguin Books Australia Ltd, Ringwood, Victoria, Australia
Penguin Books Canada Ltd, 10 Alcorn Avenue, Toronto, Ontario, Canada M4V 3B2
Penguin Books (NZ) Ltd, 182–190 Wairau Road, Auckland 10, New Zealand

Penguin Books Ltd, Registered Offices: Harmondsworth, Middlesex, England

First published in the USA by Greenwillow Books, a division of
William Morrow & Company, Inc. 1991
First published in Great Britain by Viking 1993
1 3 5 7 9 10 8 6 4 2

Text and illustrations copyright © Kevin Henkes, 1991

The moral right of the author/illustrator has been asserted

Printed in Hong Kong

A CIP catalogue record for this book is available from the British Library

ISBN 0–670–84320–2

The day she was born was the happiest day
in her parents' lives.
"She's perfect," said her mother.
"Absolutely," said her father.
And she was.
She was absolutely perfect.

"Her name must be everything she is," said her mother.

"Her name must be absolutely perfect," said her father.

And it was.

Chrysanthemum. Her parents named her Chrysanthemum.

Chrysanthemum grew and grew and grew.
And when she was old enough to appreciate it,
Chrysanthemum loved her name.

She loved the way it sounded when her mother woke her up.
She loved the way it sounded when her father called her for dinner.
And she loved the way it sounded when she whispered it to herself in the bathroom mirror.
Chrysanthemum, Chrysanthemum, Chrysanthemum.

Chrysanthemum loved the way her name looked when it was written with ink on an envelope.

She loved the way it looked when it was written with icing on her birthday cake.

And she loved the way it looked when she wrote it herself with her fat orange crayon.

Chrysanthemum, Chrysanthemum, Chrysanthemum.

Chrysanthemum thought her name was absolutely perfect.
And then she started school.

On the first day, Chrysanthemum wore her sunniest dress
and her brightest smile. She ran all the way.
"Hooray!" said Chrysanthemum. "School!"

But when Mrs Chud took the register, everyone giggled upon hearing Chrysanthemum's name.

"It's so *long*," said Jo.

"It scarcely fits on your name tag," said Rita, pointing.

"I'm named after my grandmother," said Victoria.

"You're named after a *flower*!"

Chrysanthemum wilted.

She did not think her name was absolutely perfect.

She thought it was absolutely dreadful.

The rest of the day was not much better.

During rest time Victoria raised her hand and informed
Mrs Chud that Chrysanthemum's name was spelt with
thirteen letters.

"That's exactly half as many letters as there are in the *entire*
alphabet!" Victoria explained.

"Thank you for sharing that with us, Victoria," said
Mrs Chud. "Now put your head down."

"If l had a name like yours, I'd change it," Victoria said
as the pupils lined up to go home.
I wish l could, thought Chrysanthemum miserably.

"Welcome home!" said her mother.

"Welcome home!" said her father.

"School is no place for me," said Chrysanthemum. "My name is too long. It scarcely fits on my name tag. And I'm named after a *flower*!"

"Oh, pish," said her mother. "Your name is beautiful."

"And precious and priceless and fascinating and charming," said her father.

"It's everything you are," said her mother.

"Absolutely perfect," said her father.

Chrysanthemum felt much better after her favourite dinner
(macaroni and cheese with ketchup) and an evening filled
with hugs and kisses and games.

That night Chrysanthemum dreamt that her name was Jane.
It was an extremely pleasant dream.

The next morning Chrysanthemum wore her most comfortable jumper. She walked to school as slowly as she could.
She dragged her feet in the dirt.
Chrysanthemum, Chrysanthemum, Chrysanthemum, she wrote.

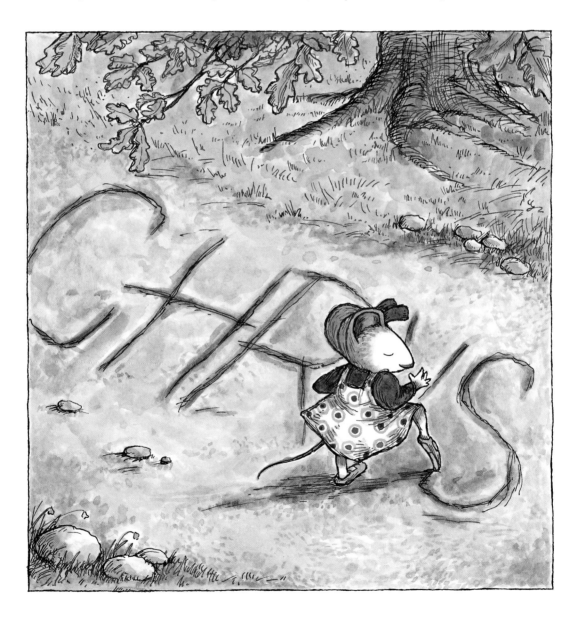

"She even *looks* like a flower," said Victoria, as
 Chrysanthemum entered the playground.
"Let's pick her," said Rita, pointing.
"Let's smell her," said Jo.

Chrysanthemum wilted.
She did not think her name was absolutely perfect.
She thought it was absolutely dreadful.

The rest of the day was not much better.

During rest time Victoria raised her hand and said,

"A chrysanthemum is a flower. It lives in a garden with worms and other dirty things."

"Thank you for sharing that with us, Victoria," said Mrs Chud.

"Now put your head down."

"I just cannot believe your name," Victoria said as the pupils
lined up to go home.
Neither can I, thought Chrysanthemum miserably.

"Welcome home!" said her mother.

"Welcome home!" said her father.

"School is no place for me," said Chrysanthemum. "They said I even *look* like a flower. They pretended to pick me and smell me."

"Oh, pish," said her mother. "They're just jealous."

"And envious and begrudging and discontented and jaundiced," said her father.

"Who wouldn't be jealous of a name like yours?" said her mother.

"After all, it's absolutely perfect," said her father.

Chrysanthemum felt a trifle better after her favourite pudding (chocolate cake with buttercream icing) and another evening filled with hugs and kisses and games.

That night Chrysanthemum dreamt that she really *was*
a chrysanthemum.

She sprouted leaves and petals. Victoria picked her and
plucked the leaves and petals one by one until there was
nothing left but a scrawny stem.

It was the worst nightmare of Chrysanthemum's life.

Chrysanthemum wore her outfit with seven pockets the
next morning.
She loaded the pockets with her most prized possessions
and her good-luck charms.
Chrysanthemum took the longest route possible to school.
She stopped and stared at each and every flower.
"Chrysanthemum, Chrysanthemum, Chrysanthemum,"
the flowers seemed to say.

That morning the students were introduced to Mrs Twinkle,
the music teacher.
Her voice was like something out of a dream, as was everything
else about her.
The pupils were speechless.
They thought Mrs Twinkle was an indescribable wonder.
They went out of their way to make a nice impression.

Mrs Twinkle led the pupils in scales.

Then she assigned roles for the class musical.

Victoria was chosen as the dainty Fairy Queen.

Rita was chosen as the spiffy Butterfly Princess.

Jo was chosen as the all-important Pixie-messenger.

And Chrysanthemum was chosen as a daisy.

"Chrysanthemum's a daisy! Chrysanthemum's a daisy!"
Jo, Rita and Victoria chanted, thinking it was wildly funny.

Chrysanthemum wilted.
She did not think her name was absolutely perfect.
She thought it was absolutely dreadful.

"What's so humorous?" asked Mrs Twinkle.

"Chrysanthemum!" was the answer.

"Her name is so *long*," said Jo.

"It scarcely fits on her name tag," said Rita, pointing.

"I'm named after my grandmother," said Victoria.

"She's named after a *flower*!"

"*My* name is long," said Mrs Twinkle.

"It is?" said Jo.

"*My* name would scarcely fit on a name tag," said Mrs Twinkle.

"It *would*?" said Rita, pointing.

"*And* –" said Mrs Twinkle, "I'm named after a flower, too!"

"You *are*?" said Victoria.

"Yes," said Mrs Twinkle. "My name is Delphinium.
   Delphinium Twinkle. And if my baby is a girl, I'm considering
   Chrysanthemum as a name. I think it's absolutely perfect."

Chrysanthemum could scarcely believe her ears.

She blushed.

She beamed.

She bloomed.

Chrysanthemum, Chrysanthemum, Chrysanthemum.

Jo, Rita and Victoria looked at Chrysanthemum longingly.

"Call me Marigold," said Jo.

"I'm Carnation," said Rita, pointing.

"My name is Lily of the Valley," said Victoria.

Chrysanthemum did not *think* her name was absolutely perfect.
She knew it!

EPILOGUE:

Overall, the class musical was a huge success.

Chrysanthemum was absolutely perfect as a daisy.

Victoria made the only mistake: she completely forgot her lines
as the dainty Fairy Queen.

Chrysanthemum thought it was wildly funny and she giggled
throughout the entire Dance of the Flowers.

Eventually, Mrs Twinkle gave birth to a healthy baby girl.
And, of course, she named her Chrysanthemum.